T0354559

PEARL

Deidre Harrison
Illustrated by Liam Ericson

Copyright © 2024 Deidre Harrison.

All rights reserved. No part of this book may be used or reproduced by any means, graphic, electronic, or mechanical, including photocopying, recording, taping or by any information storage retrieval system without the written permission of the author except in the case of brief quotations embodied in critical articles and reviews.

This is a work of fiction. All of the characters, names, incidents, organizations, and dialogue in this novel are either the products of the author's imagination or are used fictitiously.

Archway Publishing books may be ordered through booksellers or by contacting:

Archway Publishing
1663 Liberty Drive
Bloomington, IN 47403
www.archwaypublishing.com
844-669-3957

Because of the dynamic nature of the Internet, any web addresses or links contained in this book may have changed since publication and may no longer be valid. The views expressed in this work are solely those of the author and do not necessarily reflect the views of the publisher, and the publisher hereby disclaims any responsibility for them.

Any people depicted in stock imagery provided by Getty Images are models, and such images are being used for illustrative purposes only.
Certain stock imagery © Getty Images.

ISBN: 978-1-6657-6112-3 (sc)
ISBN: 978-1-6657-6111-6 (hc)
ISBN: 978-1-6657-6110-9 (e)

Library of Congress Control Number: 2024911518

Print information available on the last page.

Archway Publishing rev. date: 12/27/2024

My dedication is simply:
For my grandson Ian

Pearl opened her eyes. Something large and warm sheltered her. When she looked up, she saw large dark eyes and sharp whiskers hovering over her. The dark figure leaned down to touch Pearl's nose. Mother. Her mother.

When Pearl opened her eyes again, a watery sun shone through the fog. She was alone on a small, sandy beach. On nearby rocks, a black oystercatcher used its bright red bill to probe into mussel shells. Pearl raised her head, searching for her mother. She scanned the beach, the black rocks, and the green-gray water. Just like that, her mother emerged from a wave and popped onto the beach. With a shake, she wriggled her way up onto the dry sand until she lay next to Pearl.

Pearl snuggled up to her mother and again looked across the scattered rocky islands in the restless sea. No other seals lay on this small beach. Instead, they bunched together on one side of the largest island, mothers with small pups lying side by side, and larger seal pups tussling with their neighbors. One enormous seal, raked with scars, ignored everyone and everything, eyes closed, his nose pointing to the sky. Other seals lazed in a loose group; only Pearl and her mother lay apart.

Pearl regarded her mother with great interest. Unlike other mothers, who were mostly a dappled gray or brown, her mother was almost pure black with just the faintest of white spots, like distant stars shimmering in a night mist. Pearl herself was almost pure white with small black smudges. Mother and child were the reverse of each other.

P earl's mother nosed her. "It's time, little Pearl, to enter the sea. This beach is where we rest, but the sea is where we live." With that, Pearl's mother pulled herself to the water's edge and disappeared into a wave.

Pearl felt a moment of panic. Where did her mother go? Pearl hoisted her own small weight across the sand, marveling at her mother's effortless journey. She wiggled faster, not wanting to be left behind, until she was at the water's edge, the waves lapping around her.

Just then, her mother's head popped up, rising from the foam. "Now, little Pearl, now," she called. Pearl propelled herself forward into the water, into the shock of cold and swirling sand. Her eyes scanned the opaque world until she found her mother, shooting through the water in pursuit of darting fish.

Other seals, some with their pups, were easier to see in the water. Their coats were lighter, their actions less direct and more playful. One mother and pup rolled over and over in the water, sliding against each other in a twisty dance. Pearl's mother seemed to have no time for play. She swam away, looking backward to ensure that Pearl followed. Pearl propelled herself forward using her rear flippers, so useless on land but surprisingly powerful under water. But she couldn't hope to keep up with her mother, who disappeared into the black shadows.

After some confusing moments in the cloudy ocean, Pearl caught sight of her mother swimming toward the rocks where small fish darted and hid. She watched as her mother first flushed the fish from their hiding places and then snatched them up with her sharp, white teeth. Pearl made a few attempts to grab the silvery fish, but they easily avoided her. Soon, she felt tired.

Her mother noticed Pearl's first attempts to fish and noticed, too, that she was tiring. She nudged Pearl back toward the land. Soon the two were lifted by waves and thrown onto the small, sandy beach. Together, they made their way slowly out of the intertidal zone of low rocks, pillowy sea anemones, and pale orange sea stars, inching up onto the sand, even as the retreating tide threatened to pull Pearl back out to sea.

Once out of the waves, Pearl marveled at the soft warmth of the sand. A noontime sun hung high overhead, finally emerging from the fog. Its brilliance turned the slate-gray sea to a deep, rich blue. Pearl's mother scanned the high cliffs surrounding the beach.

"Never rest too deeply on land or at sea, little Pearl," her mother cautioned. "Danger always lurks nearby." Pearl could not picture what sort of danger her mother meant since she herself knew so little of danger. Her mother tucked her head down, and Pearl knew instinctively not to bother her with more questions.

The days passed in an easy flow of time. Pearl and her mother worked as a unit, the rhythm of their days guided by the sun above. When the sky was gray with a watery sun, Pearl's mother preferred to fish nearby. Pearl followed, smooth and sleek now. She still could not quite keep up her mother, who darted after rockfish and herring.

But she tried.

Her mother steered small silver fish in Pearl's direction, and—*snick, snack*—Pearl caught and swallowed them in one bite. These small fish, scuttling crabs, and small octopi formed most of Pearl's diet now, nearly all caught by herself. The days of lazy nursing at her mother's side were over, but Pearl did not miss them. Her mother was the best hunter, nimble and fluid, and Pearl aspired to be just like her. She relished the chase; she delighted in the sudden explosion of power needed to catch her prey. She was growing up.

Still, Pearl needed more rest than her mother, and so she often found herself alone at high tide on the warm sand while her mother fished farther out at sea on those sun-bright days. She preferred this small beach to the cold and slippery rocks, despite her mother's warnings. The other harbor seals tended to rest near each other in a clump of inert bodies. Only one very dark seal, her coat and flippers marked with long raking scars, would occasionally rest near Pearl. She had a pup with her, smaller than Pearl and very, very dark—almost as dark as Pearl's own mother. He often looked over her way before sinking his head down into the warm sand and burying his way into his mother's flank. When Pearl was with her mother, she ignored the little pup. When she was alone, however, she took care to shift herself nearer and nearer. She was curious.

One day, the little black seal was also alone.

"I'm Kelpie, and we're cousins."

Pearl had never heard this word, and she felt momentarily confused. "No, we're harbor seals."

"I know that, silly. I mean you and me. The Black Pearl is my mother's sister. Because our mothers are sisters, we are cousins. We have other cousins too. My mother told me."

"The Black Pearl?" Even as she spoke, Pearl realized this little pup was referring to her mother. She felt a momentary sense of hurt that this funny little seal knew something about her mother that she did not. "Oh, my mother. She has a sister? Are you sure? She never said anything to me."

This was not, strictly speaking, true. Pearl's mother had warned her about swimming, hunting, or resting with any of the other seals. "We're not like the others, Pearl," she had cautioned. "We have different abilities and therefore different responsibilities. I do not want you to learn their lazy ways. They are dreaming their lives away, rarely thinking about the dangers that follow us every day. I want you to focus on getting stronger and faster, little Pearl. We must ready ourselves for that danger, Pearl. We are the guardians of our own future."

Pearl looked across the water toward the far-off rocky islands. A lone harbor seal hauled herself out of the sea and onto the rocks. Pearl recognized her mother immediately—she was sleeker, stronger, and more alert than all the other harbor seals dozing blissfully under the clear blue sky. When her mother turned her gaze upon her, Pearl turned away from the nosy little pup and crashed into the waves, washing away both the sand and her questions for now.

After this, Pearl and her mother began to spend more and more time apart. The Black Pearl, as Pearl began to think of her, seemed distracted and worried, spending more time at sea. When the sea was at high tide, Pearl found herself inching closer and closer to her cousins and her aunt on the narrow strip of beach. She eavesdropped on her aunt's stories of men, of boats, of sharks, of the fierce orcas, of dogs and otters. Her aunt seemed very aware of danger. Pearl scooted in closer and closer, hungry for the lore of the sea, the lore her mother did not share with her.

"My own mother told me that the sea used to be a dark and secret place, where harbor seals and sea lions alike could hunt in the long dark columns of kelp." Pearl's Aunt Ness spoke with her eyes closed. "The kelp forest protected us and harbored our food. Sea stars came in all colors and dotted the rocks, abalone lined the crevasses along with Dungeness crabs and sea cucumbers. And the fish! They did their best to hide in the kelp, but we did have a feast every day."

P earl's aunt paused and opened her eyes, looking directly at her. "But now we must take care. The kelp forests are thinning, leaving us open to attack. Even the fishermen can easily see us swimming underneath their small boats. Sharks and orcas hunt us too. The sea has always held danger, especially for a young harbor seal like you, but we have new dangers now."

Pearl listened carefully, realizing that her aunt had been speaking more loudly than usual for her benefit. As Pearl mulled over these new ideas, she thought about her mother. They spent more and more time apart lately, with Pearl proudly catching her own small fish without her mother's help. Why had her mother never talked like this with Pearl? Pearl drifted off to sleep under the warm spring sun, filled with both curiosity and dread.

When Pearl next opened her eyes, the sun hung low in sky, and the soft gray fog was beginning to creep in. She scanned up and down the beach—most of the harbor seals Pearl knew by sight had hauled themselves out onto the dry sand, ready to rest. A few bobbed nearby in the quiet ocean, noses tilted up to breathe while they slept. But where was the Black Pearl? A sense of urgency came over Pearl—her mother had hauled out on this beach or the nearby islands every day of Pearl's short life. Where was she? In a panic, Pearl began to heave her way down to the water's edge, intent upon swimming out to look for her mother.

"Pearl. Stop," her Aunt Ness barked from behind her. "It is not safe in the water just now, little one. Your mother knows her way around a great white shark, but you do not."

Her aunt had never talked directly to Pearl before, and Pearl stopped moving out of sheer surprise. "I have to find her. She may need help."

"Your mother has never needed help, little one. She ranges farther than any seal and takes risks that most of us do not. She has always been that way. Trust her, Pearl. Trust that she knows what she is doing."

Pearl thought about her aunt's words for a moment. Deflated, she stopped where she was and began her watch.

The evening shadows lengthened and the sun glowed orange as it sank into the sea. Oystercatchers tucked their bills beneath their wings and hunkered down among black rocks. Western gulls flew to the farther offshore islands to shelter for the night. Still Pearl watched.

Once the sun had fully set, Pearl made her way sadly back to the group, nestling into the white sand, still warm with the day's heat, her nose pointed towards the sea. Before she could fall asleep, Pearl heard shuffling all around her, seals moving and murmuring between themselves.

"Black Pearl? Black Pearl. It's the Black Pearl."

Pearl raised her head to see her mother, slow and awkward, struggling to make her way up onto the beach. Even in the shadows, Pearl could see a portion of her mother's tail missing, and a deep gash in her side bleeding.

"Mother!" Pearl hurried over to the water's edge.

"The orcas are here, little one. Tell the others." Her mother's voice was strained, faint. She lay her head in the wet sand and closed her eyes.

"Orcas," barked Pearl to the others. "My mother says the orcas are here."

Her words caused the other seals to murmur unhappily. The seals who had been peacefully bobbing in the water swam in hastily. Pearl was not entirely sure what an orca was, but she remembered her aunt listing them among the many dangers of the sea. Pearl gently nudged her mother, urging her up to drier, warmer sand. Once she knew her mother was safe, Pearl lay her own head down and vowed to protect her wild, brave mother.

Sometime in the night, with the bright ceiling of stars overhead, Pearl noticed that her mother was no longer by her side. A thrill of panic coursed through her until she saw her mother in the center of the colony, bodies huddled close in, keeping her warm. Pearl felt something she had never felt before: held and protected by the colony.

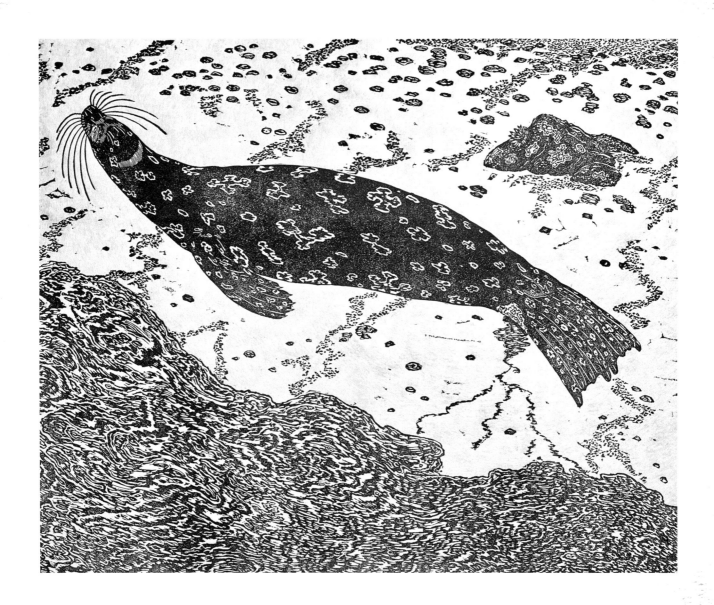

The next day arrived with rare beauty—the sky overhead was clear and cloudless, and the sea was a shifting quilt of turquoises, aquas, and deep blues. The colony began to shift and break up, some beginning to venture near the tide pools. Black Pearl raised her head and barked in a surprisingly strong voice.

"The orcas are hunting for stragglers in the gray whale's migration north. They grabbed a baby yesterday off Black Point." The harbor seals looked at one another in fear. "Her mother fought, and I tried to draw them off, but it was too late. Take care, seals. Do not venture from shore." Tired from speaking, the Black Pearl sank her head back into the sand.

"Kelpie." Pearl felt embarrassed but decided to ask. "What is an orca?"

Kelpie puffed up with pleasure at being asked. "An orca is one of our rarest but fiercest enemies. She is a whale—not a friendly whale, like the gray or the singing humpback. She is a dangerous black and white whale with huge sharp teeth. She travels in a pack, following the migrating gray whales, and tries to grab the babies. We make tasty snacks as well. Only the great white shark is more dangerous."

"Have you ever seen one?" asked Pearl.

"No, Pearl. Most seals who see an orca get eaten." Kelpie tried to sound humorous, but instead sounded anxious and sad.

"Oh," said Pearl, looking over at her exhausted mother.

As Pearl kept watch over her sleeping mother, most of the harbor seals eventually ventured out to sea, but kept near the shore, with glances toward the open ocean. Gradually, the tide began to ebb again. It was time for Pearl and her mother to relocate to the rocks off the beach. Pearl swam beside her mother, even directing a few rockfish her way, flushing them out of their hiding places. She felt gratified to see her mother snatch one or two up with something like her usual quickness. It hurt Pearl, though, to see the Black Pearl struggle awkwardly on the slick rocks. The effort broke open the wounds on her side and tail, blood mixing with the seawater coursing off her.

And then she lay still.

Still Pearl kept watch as the tide ebbed and then rose throughout the day. *It's like the ocean is breathing*, thought Pearl as she watched her mother's body rise and fall with her breath.

Kelpie's head appeared in the water below them. "How is she?"

"I don't know."

"Try not to worry, Pearl," said Kelpie "My mother says this has happened before and she always recovers. She is strong, like you are."

"But I am not strong." Pearl didn't know whether she was strong or not, but she felt like this was the right thing to say.

"No, you are. You have been swimming alongside your mother for weeks. You are the only one close to her in speed and strength, Pearl."

Pearl realized that the other seals had been discussing her, and this made her feel funny. Kelpie disappeared under the waves and Pearl watched his dark, speckled body under the clear water, darting after small fish.

"He's right, you know." The Black Pearl opened her eyes and looked directly at her daughter. "I have been training you, little Pearl, for just this. I have encouraged you to swim faster, farther, and longer than other young seals. I have been training you to take my place."

"But I don't need to take your place, Mother. Here you are. You are right here."

"Yes, little Pearl, I am here. I am here on this rock, not out in the ocean, patrolling and hunting. I am slowing down, little one, just as you are speeding up. You will soon be the fastest seal among us. And while I am healing, you are the fastest. We seal folk have always had one seal family who serve as the guardians. We are the protectors of the others, even if they never acknowledge us. We are the strongest, fastest, and most clever. And because of that, we bear the responsibility for the others."

Pearl felt a mixture of confusion and pride. She knew how often the Black Pearl had waited for her, or appeared right in front of her, silently and suddenly, knowing just where the fish were. What Pearl had not noticed until now was that no other seal could keep up with her mother, or with her. No other seals fished so far or so long out to sea.

As a pale sun began to dip into the ocean, Pearl and her mother joined the harbor seal colony assembling on the narrow beach. A soft murmur of nervous complaints competed with the lapping waves.

"How long will we have to stay so close to shore?"

"Only the littlest fish remain in this cove. With no kelp to hide in, the bigger fish are all out to sea."

"Maybe the Black Pearl was wrong. Maybe she made it all up."

"Maybe she just wants to be the hero—again."

Pearl and her mother found a spot on the sand. Pearl listened, growing angry and upset. The colony, so kind and grateful this morning, was now peevish and dissatisfied. Pearl caught Kelpie and her aunt looking at her.

"Listen here, seals," barked Aunt Ness. "The Black Pearl saved at least some of our lives yesterday by outswimming the orcas and giving us warning. Rather than showing our ingratitude with disbelief, we need to make a plan."

The other seals looked at one another, suddenly abashed.

"What about Angus? Can't he swim out and see if the orcas have gone?" piped up one young seal. The mothers all looked at one another with knowing glances.

Angus was the enormous and heavily scarred seal Pearl had noticed before. Currently he lay on one end of sandy cove, facing the sun and enjoying the last lingering warmth. During mating season, Angus fought daily, using his fierce teeth and enormous size to keep all rivals away from his seal wives. Mating season was long past now, and his wives were busy tending babies and teaching their young the ways of the sea. For Angus, his job was finished. He mostly sunned himself and swam languidly after small rockfish and octopi. Angus was no hero.

"No," said Ness, "he cannot." Angus turned his head and looked off to sea. "But Pearl can."

"The Black Pearl is injured," began one yearling.

"I'm not talking about Black Pearl. I'm talking about her daughter, Pearl."

When she heard her name mentioned, Pearl felt momentarily stunned. Swim beyond the safety of their usual grounds, looking for orcas? Only her mother could do that.

Black Pearl looked at her daughter and said, "She's right, little one. You are the only one fast enough to dare it." Pearl couldn't quite believe it, but she looked out at the wide-eyed seals, all looking back at her. She saw Kelpie nodding his head. Her heart clenched.

"Okay. I'll do it."

"And Kelpie will go with her." Ness's voice boomed.

It was Kelpie's turn to looked stunned. Then, quite suddenly, he barked, "I'll be the look-out!" In his excitement, he rocked from side to side, rolling on his fat little belly.

The Black Pearl appeared skeptical, but her sister Ness chimed in. "He's fast, too, you know. He has been following you and little Pearl farther and farther out to sea, despite my warning him not to do so. And he's sneaky." As if to prove her point, Kelpie, who had quickly and quietly scooted himself across the sand, appeared at Black Pearl's shoulder.

"I can do it, Aunt. I can."

The Black Pearl bent down to touch noses with her nephew. "Keep a look out, Kelpie, and keep her safe." Exhausted, she lay her head in the sand and closed her eyes.

The seal meeting concluded. It was decided: the young ones would swim out at dawn.

The seals broke off into small groups, some splashing into the water to find an island or do some nearby fishing for the night; others lay beached on the sand, their heads toward the sea. The murmuring continued, but Pearl could not hear what they were saying, which was probably for the best. "Kelpie, what have gotten ourselves into? I'm scared."

"I'm scared too," said Kelpie. The pale evening sun glinted in his eyes and Pearl thought she saw a tear. "I'm just glad we're going together."

"So am I," said Pearl softly.

The next morning dawned gray and cold. The warmer inland mountains had pulled the fog over the coastline like a blanket. Visibility in this weather was poor; the pale light barely penetrated the water. The four seals huddled together on the sand for last instructions.

"On your way out, swim slowly. You want to save your strength in case you have to escape in a hurry." Ness looked serious.

"And watch for fish. Notice if they are spooked by you or by something else," the Black Pearl added.

"Stay close to the small stands of kelp; think of them as hiding places."

"Whatever you do, do not become separated."

"You are dependent upon one another. No lone heroics."

Pearl and Kelpie looked at each other, eyes big. Their mothers were trying to protect them, trying to arm the youngsters with the knowledge and experience of their own long lifetimes. Each warning began to build on the next until what the two young seals were about to do began to feel huge, impossible. A silent agreement passed between Pearl and Kelpie.

"We're ready," they interrupted, in unison. They turned to splash into the water before they could change their minds.

"See you at the edge of the rocks," called Pearl.

"Right." Kelpie crashed into the waves and disappeared. Pearl looked back at her injured mother. They exchanged a long look, and then Pearl threw herself into the water and swam in the direction of Kelpie. "Eyes open," Pearl murmured to herself, "You can do this."

A few moments later, both she and Kelpie poked their heads above water, bobbing in the waves. "South?" asked Pearl.

Kelpie paused. "Might as well. We know the Black Pearl, uh, your mother, was attacked by Black Point. The orcas have probably left that area, but let's check it out." He sounded young and scared. Pearl felt scared too. "I'll go ahead," continued Kelpie, "you follow. My whiskers are humming out here. We need to look alert. I'll scan ahead, you look to the sides and occasionally look back. We don't want to be followed." Kelpie paused. "I already feel like we're being followed."

As they swam, Pearl felt astonished by this larger aquatic world, so far from their familiar beaches and coves. She marveled at the long shimmering strands of bull kelp, home to small silver fish and spiny kelp crabs. She took in the spiny purple urchins carpeting the sea floor, a few crab claws and empty abalone shells amongst them. Pearl rose to the surface, and Kelpie joined her. "So few fish. Where are the fish?"

"The sea is changing, Pearl. My mother told me that. When my mother and yours were pups, the ocean began to grow warm. Then, something happened to the sea stars—they just melted. Without the sea stars, these purple urchins began to multiply until they had eaten most the abalone. The kelp forests were next and now—well, now this is what we have."

Pearl felt stunned. "How will we eat?"

"That is why the Black Pearl has been swimming farther and farther out, trying to find the big schools of fish that used to sustain us. She found the schools—but she also found the orcas. If the orcas are still here, we'll find them too. We'll head out past Black Point to see what we can find." Kelpie looked worried.

Pearl thought of her mother, with her grave and terrible wounds. It was up to them to make sure that didn't happen to any other seal.

"I'm ready."

The water farther out was not as cloudy; Pearl could see the silver flash of anchovies ahead. Some strange harbor seals hunted out here, diving at the fish and scattering them into waiting jaws. The fishing looked good, but Pearl and Kelpie kept going.

Swimming like this—not hunting and not desperately trying to keep up with her mother—felt joyous. Pearl sped ahead, her powerful tail propelling her forward. She took a few playful loops and rolls until she noticed Kelpie, looking with attention straight ahead, intent on his task. Chastened, Pearl slowed down and joined him, looking carefully on either side, peering through the strands of bull kelp. Her whiskers hummed and she had a feeling of being watched. Kelpie suddenly stopped and Pearl held up with him. Off in the distance, Pearl could see the dull, greenish gleam of a school of salmon—a big school, moving together as one animal. Pearl had never seen this large of a school and was reminded of her hunger. If she and Kelpie didn't find the orcas, maybe they could catch a few salmon.

Cautiously, she swam toward the big school until she felt a sudden sharp nip from Kelpie. She turned to look back at him and then followed his gaze into the distance. She soon saw what Kelpie was staring at: a flash of black and white. Several small whales were swimming quickly, alertly, not like the slow and stately gray whales. As Kelpie and Pearl watched, first one, then two, and finally three orcas fiercely circled the salmon school from a distance, swimming in closer with each circle. The orcas were trying to corral the fish before the school could scatter, every fish fighting for its own survival. The orcas suddenly moved in on the salmon, which exploded in every direction, trying desperately to evade the predators. Within minutes, the orcas were coming up with great mouths full of salmon, the water suddenly blood-tinged. From their slight distance, Pearl and Kelpie both suddenly became aware of their own danger. Together, they turned and swam.

The sudden movement caught the attention of one of the orcas, an old notched and scratched female, who darted away from the wildly swimming salmon and toward the seals. Pearl saw danger coming and swam with all her strength, darting into a clump of bull kelp. Once hidden, she looked out between the long waving stalks to see the orca gaining on Kelpie, honing in on the small seal with deadly focus. Pearl gathered her courage and swam out, directly across the path between the orca and the tiring Kelpie.

The orca paused for a moment in her headlong chase of Kelpie and swung left to follow Pearl, who then saw another orca take note of the new prey. She could not afford to let them trap her, but she also had to give Kelpie a chance to escape. She led the orcas back towards the kelp forests, and found her way into the glossy, undulating ropes of kelp. The younger orca slowed and turned back towards the salmon, an easier prey. Only the old female followed her now. Pearl paused in the kelp, holding her breath and holding still, willing the orca to give up and return to her pod. Moments passed amidst the slowly waving kelp. A few rockfish swam by, lulled by Pearl's stillness into a false sense of safety. A large shadow passed over Pearl like a terrible ghost: the orca. Nothing else besides a boat or an orca could cast a shadow like that. Pearl waited and waited, still holding her breath. Where was Kelpie?

The water around her suddenly roiled with slick gray shapes, seal-shaped but not seals. The shapes rocketed though the bull kelp, leaving a trail of bubbles and shredded leaves. She felt a paralyzing sense of terror. Should she flee or stand guard, escape or continue hiding? And where, oh where, was Kelpie? The silken creatures flashed to and fro in a froth of bubbles. Strange high squeaks and squeals followed, disorienting Pearl. Her brain spun, and she began to panic. What if these were also enemies seeking to harm her or Kelpie? She swam free, straight into the explosion of bubbles, desperate to find Kelpie. She had only the vaguest idea of where the orcas were, but she had promised the older seals that she and Kelpie would stay together. She had to be brave.

Then she saw him. He was floating free from the kelp forest, where he too had been hiding, suspended in the swirling water, transported, transcendent, joyful.

Pearl looked around at the suddenly silent sea, empty of orcas, of salmon, of the gray demons, of rockfish and anchovy—empty of everything except the two of them and the scattered bits of torn kelp and swirling sand. With a silent nod, they rose to the surface. Pearl, breaking water first, was unable to shake the feeling of being followed. She scanned the surface for the slightest sign of orcas.

"Dolphins," sputtered Kelpie before his head had fully surfaced. "Risso's dolphins. Mother told me about them." Pearl once again felt her own lack of education. "They don't come very often, but they are fearless and brave and…" Kelpie could hardly contain his excitement. "And, well, they eat all the fish in the sea, says my mother. But then they leave."

"What just happened, Kelpie? Why did they make a run right for the orcas?"

"I think they saved us," said Kelpie. "I don't know much about them, but Mother calls them tricksters, untrustworthy renegades. They stick to themselves and have their own language." Kelpie paused. "But I think they must be angels. Look around; they've led the orcas away. We're safe."

Indeed, as Pearl scanned farther out to sea, she could see a roil of water far away, growing more distant all the time. The orca pod had taken off after the dolphins.

"Will they be okay, Kelpie?"

Kelpie laughed as he bobbed in the sea. "Oh, I think so. They are amazing—so fast, so smart." Privately, Pearl thought he sounded like a seal in love.

As Pearl and Kelpie made their way back to their familiar beach, they began to see fish emerging from under rocks and from behind the kelp where they had been hiding. They still darted away from the young harbor seals, but sensing the seals were not on a hunting mission, kept just out of reach. Pearl searched each clump of kelp, still anxious about being followed.

"Kelpie! Pearl!" Ness was waiting on the thin band of high tide beach. She huffed her way into the surf, touching noses, first with Kelpie and then with Pearl, as both collapsed onto the sand. Pearl scanned the narrow beach for her mother, without seeing her anywhere.

"I tried to stop her." Her aunt's voice sounded anguished. "She went out to watch over you both."

Pearl refused to leave the beach that night—even when the other seals stationed themselves on the offshore rocks, high above the tide, or fished silently in the calm waters. Kelpie refused to leave her side.

"She's my mother and I will wait for her here. She's still so weak." Pearl knew it was risky for a lone seal on the beach at night. She had learned from her Aunt Ness that she could ignore the river otters from the nearby streams patrolling the shore, prying mussels off low rocks. She could not ignore the bobcats, mountain lions, and coyotes waiting for their chance at an injured or inattentive seal. If her mother beached during the night, she wanted to be there to protect her.

Pearl hadn't meant to fall asleep, but the excitement and terror of the previous day had been too much. She and Kelpie both nodded off. When she stirred a few hours later, a raccoon stood on its hind legs to look at her and then scurried off with a shiny blue mussel in its mouth. No sign of the bigger and more lethal predators.

A dark shape lay farther down the beach. Although it looked like nothing more than a waterlogged piece of driftwood or a fat clump of kelp, Pearl set off across the beach, lumbering awkwardly. As she came closer, she realized it was her mother. The Black Pearl lay utterly still, blood oozing anew from the old wounds, and only the shallowest rise and fall of her body indicating breath and life.

"Mother. Oh, Mother." Pearl nosed her mother and was rewarded by seeing her eyes flicker and then open.

"My Pearl," she said, weakly. "You are safe."

Pearl suddenly knew that her feeling of being followed had been true. She and Kelpie had been followed by her mother.

"You were out there with us. Oh, Mother, you should not have. You've hurt yourself again."

"I couldn't let you face such danger alone," came the soft reply.

"But I had Kelpie, and then the dolphins—did you see them?" Despite her fear and concern for her mother, Pearl felt a thrill of happiness when she mentioned the dolphins. Angels, Kelpie called them.

"I did see them, little Pearl. They are brave and reckless, but you are braver still." The effort to talk taxed the little strength the Black Pearl had left.

"Come up on the sand, Mother, and rest." Pearl's heart broke watching her mother struggle even to speak.

"I have something important to tell you, little one. I need to tell you that I have been wrong. I counseled you to stay away from the others, to look only to develop yourself and your own speed. I told you to avoid other seals because they were not of the guardian line. I told you that you and I are faster, smarter, stronger, as if somehow that made us better. As if, somehow, that made us not need others. But I know now that was wrong and I'm sorry."

"I know, Mother," said Pearl softly. "I found that out. Kelpie is my best friend and Auntie Ness has been teaching me too. The other seals have—mostly—been very kind. But we need to get you out to a rock to rest. It will be safer there." Pearl scanned the cliffs for coyotes, dogs, or humans. "It's dangerous for you here."

Then, Kelpie was by her side. "Auntie, let's get you off the beach."

The sad trio inched their way towards the waves, Black Pearl leaving a trail of blood and wincing with each movement.

"You're almost there, Mother. We're both here, and we will swim with you."

The three seals plunged into the water, feeling the safety and support it provided. Pearl and Kelpie steered Black Pearl to a set of low-lying rocks, slick with eelgrass, but watched helplessly as she tried to hoist herself up out of the water. She tried again and again, but each time, she sank back down into the water. Finally, they all returned to the beach. Pearl could see that her mother had used every last bit of her strength.

"Mother, I will stay here and protect you."

The Black Pearl opened one eye and shook her head. "No, you are in danger here."

Ness had appeared on the beach as well, and now she looked down, thoughtful. "Let's take turns. You two need to eat."

Pearl began to protest but her mother said in a surprisingly strong voice, "Listen to your aunt. Go off and eat now, Pearl. Go, Kelpie." Pearl opened her mouth to protest further but Kelpie shook his head.

"We're going to upset her if we don't go, Pearl."

So off they went, plunging into the waves, Pearl determined to be back as soon as possible with a rockfish in her mouth for her mother.

Fishing was good, and Pearl snapped up a few small cod and crunched open a Dungeness crab. She soon lost track of Kelpie, last seen chasing a rockfish. When she was full, Pearl swan back toward the beach. Emerging from a wave with a fat greenling in her mouth, she started in surprise. Only Kelpie and her Aunt Ness rested on the beach, alone.

"Where is my mother?"

"She's gone," said Ness sadly. "We tried to stop her, but she was determined."

"Gone? Gone where?" Pearl looked up and down the beach. "She's too weak."

"That's just what she said. That she's too weak. I think she's gone where we are not meant to find her." Kelpie's unhappiness was evident in the downward droop of his whiskers. "I tried to stop her, I promise. I really tried."

Pearl gazed sadly out to sea; her heart broken into a thousand jagged pieces. She knew her mother well, and as the gravity of Kelpie's words sunk in, those thousand pieces broke into a thousand more. Her mother was gone.

Epilogue

Pearl swam slowly and carefully, looking back over her shoulder at the tiny black seal trailing her, its little tail pumping madly. In the years since her mother disappeared, Pearl had matured into the fastest and strongest of the harbor seals, a well-respected guardian and leader. When it was her time, she gave birth to her own little seal, a feisty coal black pup called Onyx whose coat shimmered with faint bursts of white, just like the Black Pearl. Already, she promised to be as fast and as smart as her mother, as her grandmother, as her aunt and as her cousin Kelpie. Onyx would surely be wise and observant like Kelpie, who had grown into a sleek and powerful seal with a family of his own, but who took an active interest in his little cousin. Pearl watched as her daughter darted after the small silver anchovies and reddish-brown octopi, not catching a single one. Not yet.

As Pearl watched Onyx, she felt herself being watched. She had had this feeling ever since her mother disappeared that terrible day several seasons ago. When she told her aunt about this feeling, Ness cautioned her. "Pearl, please don't get your hopes up. I'm afraid my sister, the Black Pearl, is gone."

But Pearl herself wasn't sure. She had become as great a hunter and scout as her mother had been. She trusted her instincts and she knew when they were telling her of danger and when they were not. This sensation of being watched did not feel like danger. It did not feel menacing or frightening.

It felt comforting. It felt like safety. It felt like love.

About the Author

Deidre Harrison is an educator, nature lover, and grandmother. She lives in Northern California with her husband and her Labradoodle Maeve.

Printed in the United States
by Baker & Taylor Publisher Services